I Learn from My Cousins

Amy Rogers

illustrated by
Anita Morra

PowerKiDS press.

New York

Published in 2018 by The Rosen Publishing Group, Inc.
29 East 21st Street, New York, NY 10010

First Edition

Managing Editor: Nathalie Beullens-Maoui
Editor: Greg Roza
Art Director: Michael Flynn
Book Design: Raúl Rodriguez
Illustrator: Anita Morra

Cataloging-in-Publication Data

Names: Rogers, Amy B., author.
Title: I learn from my cousins / Amy Rogers.
Description: New York : PowerKids Press, [2018] | Series: The things I learn | Includes index.
Identifiers: LCCN 2017013183| ISBN 9781538327128 (pbk. book) | ISBN
  9781538327845 (6 pack) | ISBN 9781508163770 (library bound book)
Subjects: LCSH: Cousins–Juvenile literature. | Family recreation–Juvenile
  literature.
Classification: LCC HQ759.97 .R64 2018 | DDC 306.87–dc23
LC record available at https://lccn.loc.gov/2017013183

Manufactured in the United States of America

CPSIA Compliance Information: Batch #BW18PK. For further information contact Rosen Publishing, New York, New York at 1-800-237-9932

Contents

I'm always learning!
My cousins help me
learn new things.

5

My cousins Bailey and Shawn
are great teachers.

They teach me things at the park.

We love the swings.

Shawn and Bailey teach me how to
move my legs to swing high.

There are baby ducks at the park.
Shawn says they're called ducklings.

My cousins help me count
the ducklings.

We count seven
of them!

Bailey brought her jump rope.

She teaches me
how to use it.

Bailey teaches me to share
the jump rope with Shawn.

I want to go on the slide.

Shawn says we have to wait our turn.

Bailey says to wait until the boy before
me is out of the way.

Then I fly down the slide!

It's fun to learn with Bailey and Shawn!

Words to Know

jump rope

slide

swings

Index

D
ducklings, 11, 12

J
jump rope, 14, 16

P
park, 7, 11

S
share, 16